GOOD DOG, CARL

By
Alexandra Day

Aladdin Paperbacks

To H.D., who has never let us forget about Ponies

First Aladdin Paperbacks edition August 1997
Copyright © 1985 by Alexandra Day

Aladdin Paperbacks
An imprint of Simon & Schuster Children's Publishing Division
1230 Avenue of the Americas, New York, NY 10020

Also available in a Simon & Schuster Books for Young Readers edition.
22 24 26 28 30 29 27 25 23
Library of Congress Cataloging-in-Publication Data

Day, Alexandra
Good dog, Carl / by Alexandra Day.
— 1st Aladdin Paperbacks ed.
p.   cm.
Summary: Lively and unusual things happen when
Carl the dog is left in charge of the baby.
ISBN-13: 978-0-689-81771-7 (pbk.)   ISBN-10: 0-689-81771-1 (pbk.)
[1. Babies—Fiction. 2. Dogs—Fiction.
3. Babysitters—Fiction. 4. Stories without words.]
1. Title
PZ7.D32915Gp   1997 [E]—dc21
97-18516 CIP AC
Manufactured in China
0512 SCP

"Look after the baby, Carl.
I'll be back shortly."

"Good dog, Carl!"

A salute to the creator of Münchener Bilderbogen No. 1001,
and thanks to Molly Myers and Toby for their sitting talent.

The paintings for this book were executed in egg tempera.
Color separations by Photolitho, AG, Gossau/Zurich, Switzerland.
Printed and bound in China.